Vanessa
the Dance Steps
Fairy

For Bethany Ann and Megan Rose Middleton-Hunt, with lots of love

Special thanks to
Sue Mongredien

ORCHARD BOOKS
338 Euston Road, London NW1 3BH
Orchard Books Australia
Level 17/207 Kent Street, Sydney, NSW 2000
A Paperback Original

First published in 2012 by Orchard Books

A CIP catalogue record for this book is available
from the British Library.

ISBN 978 1 40831 591 0

1 3 5 7 9 10 8 6 4 2

Printed in Great Britain

The paper and board used in this paperback are natural recyclable
products made from wood grown in sustainable forests. The
manufacturing processes conform to the environmental regulations
of the country of origin.

Orchard Books is a division of Hachette Children's Books,
an Hachette UK company

www.hachette.co.uk

Vanessa
the Dance Steps Fairy

by Daisy Meadows

ORCHARD

www.rainbowmagic.co.uk

Fairyland Music Festival
A-OK trailer
Rehearsal tent
Star Village
Picnic hill
Beach

Jack Frost's Ice Castle

Camping site

Girls' tent

Main Stage

Karaoke tent

Cafe

The Harbour

Rainspell Island

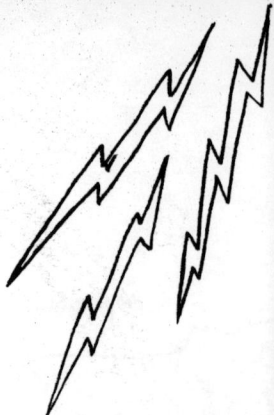

Jack Frost's Spell

It's high time for the world to see
The legend I was born to be.
The prince of pop, a dazzling star
My fans will flock from near and far.

But pop star fame is hard to get
Unless I help myself, I bet.
I need a plan, a cunning trick
To make my stage act super-slick.

Seven magic clefs I'll steal
They'll give me pop star powers, I feel.
I'll sing and dance, I'll dazzle and shine
And pop star glory will be mine!

Contents

Festival Fun

"Hooray!" cheered Rachel Walker, as she and her best friend Kirsty Tate walked on to Rainspell Beach. "The sun is shining, we're on holiday together *and* we're at the Rainspell Island Music Festival."

"It's been wonderful so far, hasn't it?" Kirsty agreed with a smile.

It was certainly turning out to be a day the girls would never forget. First, they'd seen their favourite band, The Angels, open the show. Next to perform were the boy band, A-OK, who'd wowed the crowd with their melodic harmonies. And best of all, Kirsty and Rachel had found themselves caught up in an exciting new fairy adventure, this time with the Pop Star Fairies!

"Hi, girls," came three familiar voices just then.

Rachel and Kirsty turned to see Lexy, Serena and Emilia – also known as The Angels.

"Hi," beamed Kirsty. She and Rachel had met the band before when they'd helped Destiny the Pop Star Fairy, and were lucky enough to have backstage passes to the festival. Being friends with pop stars was almost as much fun as being friends with the fairies!

"Did you see A-OK? Weren't they fab?" said Lexy.

"I didn't know they were such great performers," said Emilia, kicking off her sandals and wiggling her bare toes in the golden sand.

"Those boys rocked!"

"I can't wait to see Sasha Sharp tonight," Rachel put in. "She's a brilliant dancer."

"Sasha's amazing," Serena agreed. "Have you seen the video to her new song, *Let's Dance*? She does such a cool routine. How does it go again?"

The Angels started singing Sasha's latest hit, and they all tried to remember the dance moves.

"Up, down, spin around and touch the ground,
Come on, everybody! Let's dance around town.
With a hop to the left and a jump to the right,
Come on, everybody! Let's dance tonight."

It was hard dancing on the sand though. It wasn't long before Kirsty and Rachel bumped into each other and fell over.

"Whoops!" giggled Kirsty, brushing sand off her clothes. "I think we need some practice, Rachel."

"Well, there's a dance class starting soon in Star Village if you want to join in," Serena told them. Star Village was a cluster of tents in the festival site where you could try out all sorts of pop star activities – dance, fashion design, make-up and singing lessons.

Lexy winked. "I've heard there's going to be a special surprise there actually," she added mysteriously.

Kirsty and Rachel looked at one another. "Let's go!" they said in the same breath.

The two friends said goodbye to The Angels and hurried towards the dance tent. It was late in the afternoon now and the sun was sinking through the sky. The festival was as busy as ever, with delicious smells of hot dogs and burgers wafting from food vans, and lots of stalls selling clothes and jewellery.

"I wonder what the surprise will be," Rachel said. "We've already had so many other exciting surprises today, I can't imagine what else could possibly happen."

Rachel was right – the girls had
had one surprise after another since
they'd come to Rainspell Island that
morning. First they'd been whisked
off to Fairyland by Destiny, who'd
invited them to watch the rehearsals
for the Fairyland Music Festival. It was
wonderful to be back in Fairyland, but
unfortunately the rehearsals hadn't gone
to plan. Mean Jack Frost had stolen the
Pop Star Fairies' seven magical clefs,
which helped ensure that pop stars
performed perfectly everywhere. Without
their clefs, even the Pop Star Fairies
didn't sound or look good any more.

Jack Frost wanted to become a pop
star himself and had taken the clefs to
the Rainspell Festival so that he could
use their powers. So far the girls had

helped Jessie the Lyrics Fairy and Adele the Singing Coach Fairy get their clefs back from Jack Frost's goblins who were looking after them, but five were still missing. If Kirsty and Rachel couldn't find them in time, the festival might be ruined.

"This has definitely been one of the most exciting days of my life," Kirsty said as they reached Star Village. "I can't wait to see what happens next!"

A Dance Disaster

Rachel and Kirsty found the large dance tent and went inside.

"Hi there," said a friendly lady. She had corkscrew curls held back with a swirly-patterned hairband, and wore a purple leotard and leggings. "I'm Tamara, Sasha Sharp's assistant. Welcome to our dance class."

"Hi," Rachel said. "Do we need to wear special clothes for the class?" she asked, noticing that lots of children had arrived in leotards and little dance skirts. Others were sitting on the floor trying on dance shoes.

"No," Tamara said, "but you can borrow some dance shoes if you want. Help yourselves." She led them to a rack full of shoes in all colours. Kirsty chose a lilac pair, and Rachel found some bright pink ones.

There were small 'shoe mirrors' dotted around the tent so that you could see how they looked.

The girls went to a quiet corner, and took off their sandals. Kirsty was just about to slip her foot into her dance shoe when there was a bright flash of colour… and to her surprise, a little fairy fluttered out in a shower of rainbow-coloured fairy dust! "Oh!" Kirsty gasped. "Hello there."

Rachel and Kirsty had met all seven of the Pop Star Fairies and recognised Vanessa the Dance Steps Fairy because of her lilac trilby

hat. She was also wearing a short blue playsuit with crossover straps and pink lace-up dance shoes with a chunky heel. "Hello," Rachel said excitedly. "How are you? Have you found your magic clef yet?"

Vanessa shook her head. "No," she said. "And look what's been happening without it!"

She waved her wand at one of the small shoe mirrors and with a flurry of green sparkles, a scene appeared.

22

The girls recognised the Fairyland Music Festival stage, then saw the Dance Fairies walk on to begin their rehearsal. Kirsty and Rachel knew what talented dancers the Dance Fairies were — but not today. The scene in the mirror showed them crashing into each other, tripping over and dancing out of time.

"Oh dear," Rachel said, wincing as Saskia the Salsa Fairy fell off the stage.

"They're even worse than we were on the beach," Kirsty said, remembering how they'd fallen over.

Vanessa gave a sigh. "I'm worried about Sasha Sharp's performance," she said. "If I don't get my magical clef back in time, she'll be dancing badly too – and so will everyone else at the festival."

Before the girls had a chance to reply, they heard Tamara's voice. "OK, everyone, our special class is about to begin," she announced. "Please could you form rows in front of the stage? This way!"

Kirsty looked round to see a raised stage at the far end of the tent. "I guess we should go," she said.

"Vanessa, why don't you hide in my pocket?" Rachel suggested, pulling it open so that the little fairy could flutter inside. "We'll keep an eye out for your clef."

Rachel and Kirsty lined up with the other children, although there was still no sign of the dance teacher. Then the lights dimmed, and plumes of hissing purple smoke poured from the side of the stage. A single spotlight appeared revealing the shadowy shape of a dancer wearing a leotard, a big shiny belt and high heels.

Music blasted out and Kirsty recognised the catchy opening to Sasha Sharp's song *Let's Dance*. A huge cheer went up.

"Up, down, spin around and touch the ground…" went the song, and on the word 'up', the dancer on stage leapt high into the air. Unfortunately, she fell awkwardly and tumbled right off the stage, landing at Kirsty and Rachel's feet with a thump.

"Oh gosh, are you all right?" Rachel gasped, bending down to help her up.

At that moment, the music stopped and the lights came on again. As the tent was flooded with brightness, the girls realised, to their great surprise, that the dancer was none other than Sasha Sharp herself!

A gasp went around as the other children recognised her too. Sasha gave a shaky laugh and got up, with Rachel and Kirsty both helping her. "Thanks, guys," she said. Then she smiled sheepishly at the audience.

"That was a lesson in how *not* to start your dance routine… especially as I'm hoping some of you will join me on stage tonight, as my backing dancers!"

There was stunned silence for a second… and then the tent erupted with excitement. Some girls were screaming and clutching each other. Others, like Rachel and Kirsty, jumped up and down cheering. This must be the surprise The Angels had been talking about!

"You're serious? You're really going to have some of us on stage for your concert?" Kirsty asked Sasha in delight. The festival was getting better and better!

Sasha grinned. "Oh yes," she said. "Cool surprise, huh?"

"The best!" Rachel laughed. How she hoped that she and Kirsty would be picked to dance!

"Okay," Sasha said, clambering back onstage. "So let's practise. Copy me and we'll see how we get on. Are we ready with the music? One, two, three… hit it!"

The opening notes of *Let's Dance* sounded through the tent once more and everyone copied Sasha's starting position. Rachel and Kirsty watched carefully as the famous pop star led them through the routine. It wasn't too complicated, but unfortunately, however hard they tried, everyone, even Sasha, kept making mistakes.

"I don't know what's wrong with me today," she grumbled as she lost her balance for the third time. "I've danced this routine so many times I thought I could do it in my sleep."

Rachel heard Vanessa sigh from where she was still tucked in her pocket. "It's because my magical clef is missing," she murmured. "We have to get it back, otherwise Sasha and her dancers are going to be in all kinds of trouble tonight!"

Here Come the Boys

"Let's have another try," Sasha said wearily. "From the top!"

The rehearsal began once more, but it quickly turned into chaos yet again. Some people leaped up when they should be crouching down, while others jumped sideways when they should have been spinning around. Just as the whole thing was starting to look hopeless, four boys arrived late to the class and joined in.

They were wearing bright green leotards and large feathery hats that covered their faces.

"They're good," Kirsty hissed, noticing their graceful movements.

The boys *were* good, Rachel thought, stopping to watch – much better than anyone else there. They leaped high on the word 'up', landed perfectly on the word 'down', then gracefully spun round and touched the ground each time.

As the song finished, the rest of
the crowd clapped the boys, and so
did Sasha. "Hey! You guys did that
perfectly," she cheered. "Way better
than I've been dancing, that's for sure."
She leaned down and rubbed her ankle,
wincing. Clearly it was still hurting from
where she'd fallen on it before.

Tamara had noticed that Sasha was in pain, and joined her on stage. "OK, everyone, now it's down to you to practise," she called out. "Meet back here at six o'clock for a final rehearsal."

The children began filing out of the tent, still humming the song and chattering excitedly about the show that evening. Kirsty and Rachel put their sandals back on, as Sasha limped to the side of the stage. Tamara, meanwhile, was briskly gathering up the pop star's belongings.

With various costumes and pairs of
shoes, as well as Sasha's handbag, there
was a lot to carry.

"Can we help?" Rachel offered.

"If we carry your
things, Tamara
could support
you,
Sasha,"
Kirsty
suggested
politely.

"Thank
you, girls,"
Sasha said.
"That would be very
kind. I'll have to rest my foot and just
hope it gets better quickly. The show
must go on!"

The four of them went back to the star's trailer, which was painted a bright turquoise and decorated with pink and purple butterflies. Once inside, Sasha sank gratefully into an armchair, while Tamara hung up the costumes. "We'll get you a drink," Rachel suggested, seeing the little kitchen through a doorway.

Sasha smiled. "Thank you," she said. "You're both angels, looking after me like this."

In the kitchen, Kirsty found a glass and filled it with cold water. Vanessa, meanwhile, fluttered out of Rachel's pocket and waved her wand. "This will help Sasha's ankle," she said, as an ice-pack magically appeared in Rachel's hand.

"Good idea," Rachel whispered, as Vanessa darted back to her hiding place. "Thank goodness for fairy magic!"

She and Kirsty took the drink and ice-pack to Sasha who thanked them again. "That feels good," she sighed as Tamara put the ice-pack on her swollen ankle.

"The sooner I can start practising again the better. I don't know *what* was wrong with me earlier. I can't understand it. If I dance that badly tonight, my fans are going to be really disappointed."

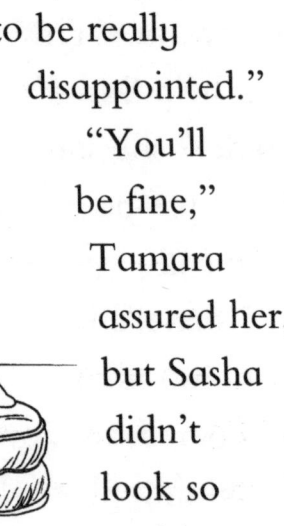

"You'll be fine," Tamara assured her, but Sasha didn't look so confident.

"I hope you feel better soon," Kirsty said. "We'd better go and practise the routine ourselves now. We'll see you later."

Once they were outside the trailer, the three friends exchanged worried looks. "I'm not feeling very hopeful about tonight," Rachel sighed. "We haven't got long before Sasha's show, and there's still no sign of your clef, Vanessa."

"Those boys were good in the dance class, weren't they?" Kirsty remembered. "You don't suppose…"

The thought occurred to them all at the same time. "They were goblins!" they chorused.

"They were dancing so well, one of them must be wearing my magic dance clef," Vanessa realised. "There's no time to lose – we've got to find those goblins!"

Kirsty Has a Plan

Vanessa waved her wand at the girls
and a stream of green stars swirled out
from its tip. In the next moment, Kirsty
and Rachel had shrunk down to the
size of fairies… and had their very own
shimmering wings. "Let's fly!" Vanessa
said, grinning at their delighted faces.
She zoomed into the air, and Kirsty and
Rachel followed, loving the feeling of
soaring so fast above the festival crowds.

They flew around Star Village, where
they'd last seen the goblins, hoping to
spot them again. But although there
were lots of people in the different tents,
the three fairy friends couldn't see any
sign of the goblins
at all.

"Maybe
they're
practising
their dance
routines
backstage,"
Rachel
suggested.

"Let's look there."
But despite searching all round the
main stage and the backstage area, there
was no sign of the goblins there either.

In fact, even after flying around the pop stars' trailers and rehearsal tents, and all the way through the campsite, they still hadn't found them. "We've searched everywhere. Where can they be?" Kirsty said, frowning.

Just then, they heard a faint musical beat. "Someone's listening to *Let's Dance*," Rachel said, recognising the tune.

"And the music's coming from Rainspell Beach," Vanessa realised. "Let's look there!"

It was breezy down on the beach, and the three fairies had to battle against the wind to fly. But it was worth the struggle. Within minutes, they'd tracked the sound of the music along the sand, then saw the goblins practising their dance moves at the far end of the beach. They'd brought along an MP3 player with speakers and were all dancing perfectly in time.

"Let's hide behind these rocks and watch," Kirsty suggested, ducking down out of sight. Rachel and Vanessa followed, then they all peeped out to watch the dancers.

The goblins were taking it in turns
to dance solos, with athletic jumps and
spins. "Woohoo!" one goblin cheered at
the end of his routine. "Dancing is much
more fun than being bossed around by
Jack Frost."

"My turn!" another goblin announced
impatiently. He snatched something from
the first goblin, and Rachel stiffened as
she caught a glimpse of it. Vanessa's
magical clef!

"Did you see that?" she whispered excitedly to Kirsty and Vanessa. "The clef!"

"Yes," Vanessa beamed. "Let's try to think of a way to get it back."

The goblins were all fighting over the clef – pushing each other and grabbing at it. "They're so busy fighting, they might not notice if a couple more goblins join in," Kirsty said thoughtfully. "Vanessa, do you think you could you magic me and Rachel into goblins?"

"Of course!" Vanessa said, waving her wand. Another flood of fairy dust sparkled around Kirsty and Rachel and then, in the next moment, they found themselves growing taller… and greener!

Now Rachel and Kirsty looked just like goblins, complete with the same leotards as the four goblin dancers, who were still wrestling and making a dreadful row.

49

"You'll have to be quick," Vanessa warned. "My magic isn't at full strength without my clef. The disguises won't last long."

"Then there's no time to lose," said Kirsty, her heart thumping. "Let's go!"

Rachel and Kirsty hurried over to the fighting goblins and joined in the noisy scrum, hoping to grab the clef.

The goblins were pushing and shoving as fiercely as ever, and Kirsty narrowly avoided being elbowed in the face.
The sooner they saw the clef the better, Rachel thought, as she was jostled by a sharp goblin elbow.

Then Kirsty spotted that the clef had been dropped on the sand and dived down to get it.

She was just fighting her way back out again when a tall skinny goblin saw her holding the clef and promptly tripped her over.

The clef went flying out of Kirsty's hand – but by a stroke of luck, Rachel managed a brilliant catch. Now *she* had it!

Not for long. A thick-set goblin with an enormous wart on his nose grabbed it from her fingers. And as Rachel saw the clef vanish from her grasp, she saw something else vanishing too…

her goblin disguise! Vanessa's magic was obviously wearing off already. She and Kirsty had to get back to their hiding place before the goblins realised who they really were!

Dance-Off Drama

Rachel nudged Kirsty and pointed out what was happening. Then both girls dashed for the safety of the rocks, just in time. By the time they'd crouched down out of sight, the last tinges of green had faded from their skin, and they were their normal selves again.

"Oh dear," Kirsty whispered. "That didn't work as well as I hoped."

"It's getting close to six," Vanessa said, fluttering to land on Rachel's wrist and peeping at her watch. "The goblins will be going back to the dance tent soon to find Tamara and Sasha for the rehearsal. We must think of something quickly."

Vanessa's words about the rehearsal gave Rachel an idea. "Vanessa, do you think you could use your magic to make one of us look like Tamara this time?" she asked.

She quickly explained her plan to them, and both Kirsty and Vanessa smiled. "I love it!" Kirsty said. "Great thinking. Shall I be Tamara?"

Vanessa looked anxiously at her wand. "I don't have a lot of magic left," she said. "Disguising Kirsty as Tamara and magicking you back to fairy-size, Rachel, is going to use up the last bit of power – so we've got to get this right. Otherwise…"

She didn't finish her sentence, but she didn't need to. Both Rachel and Kirsty knew that this was their last chance. "We'll give it our best shot," Rachel promised.

Vanessa waved her wand and more
of her sparkly magic poured out. There
was just enough to turn Rachel back
into a fairy, and to make Kirsty look like
Tamara, with curly hair and a purple
leotard. The magic also gave her a shiny
gold cup to hold.

"In you get," Kirsty laughed, holding

out the cup, and
Vanessa and
Rachel both flew
down inside.

"Give us the
signal when
you need
us," Rachel
reminded Kirsty
in a whisper.
"And good luck!"

"Thanks," Kirsty whispered back.
"Here goes." And she walked out from
behind the rocks, straight up to the
fighting goblins.

"Hi, boys," she said to them.
"Remember me? I'm Tamara, Sasha
Sharp's assistant."

The goblins stopped fighting
immediately and stared in surprise.

"We're looking for new talent, and we both thought you danced brilliantly at the class today," Kirsty went on. "In fact, Sasha thought one of you should have an award for such awesome dancing. The question is, who deserves it the most?"

There was a moment of stunned silence as the goblins took in this exciting news, and then they all shouted at once. "Me! I'm the best!"

"I should get the cup!"

"I can do a triple spin – on my head!"

"Whoa, whoa!"
Kirsty said,
to the noisy
goblins.
"There's only
one way to
decide this.
We'll have
a dance-off –
and the winner
will be awarded
this trophy. Who's going first?"

Peeping over the edge of the cup, Rachel noticed that one goblin had the magical clef wrapped around his wrist on a chain. He was smirking. "I am so going to win this," he laughed to the others. "You might as well let me have the cup now!"

"That's not fair, you can't wear the clef for the dance-off," the warty-nosed goblin grumbled.

"Yeah, take it off," a third goblin said bossily. "Otherwise you're not allowed to take part."

"All right, all right," grumbled the goblin with the clef. He took it from his wrist and made a show of leaving it on the sand. But then, while the other goblins weren't looking, he tucked the clef quickly into the sequinned belt around his leotard.

"Are we ready? Let's have our first dancer," Kirsty said, and pressed a button on the MP3 player to start the music.

The tallest goblin began to dance while the others watched. "He's not *awful*," Rachel whispered to Vanessa as they both peered out. "But he definitely danced better when he had the clef."

Vanessa nodded. "His dancing is quite good because he's near the clef," she explained in a whisper.

"The closer they are to it, the better they'll be."

Then came the second dancer who also danced well... until one of the other goblins slyly stuck out his foot and tripped him up. He fell in a heap on the sand, looking furious. "That's cheating," he grumbled sulkily, and refused to try again.

Next was the dancer who'd secretly tucked the clef in his belt... and he was *amazing*. He twirled and spun, he hopped and jumped, performing a string of complicated and difficult moves with a big smile on his face. Clearly he was having a lot of fun showing off to an audience!

As he danced, the clef slid out from where he'd hid it, and dangled temptingly from his belt. Rachel exchanged a glance with Vanessa. "Shall we?" she whispered.

"Let's!" Vanessa whispered in reply.

Stage Magic

The two fairies sneaked out of the golden cup, and sped towards the dancing goblin, trying to get close enough to grab the clef without being spotted. It wasn't easy – the goblin was flinging himself around so swiftly that Rachel started to feel dizzy from racing about after him.

Round and round she and Vanessa flew, and Rachel was just beginning to feel as if she'd never get near the clef when the track ended and the goblin struck a dramatic pose. Quick as lightning, Rachel made a dive for the musical clef and pulled it from the goblin's belt. She passed it to Vanessa, and the clef immediately shrank down to its usual fairy size with a bright flash of sparkles. Hurrah – they'd done it!

The two fairies flew a safe distance from the goblin, beaming in delight.

The goblin, meanwhile, hadn't realised
the clef was gone and began dancing
to the next tune. Of course, without the
clef, he wasn't anywhere near as skilful,
and he tripped over his big green feet
within seconds.

Just then,
Kirsty's
disguise as
Tamara
began
to wear
off and the
goblins gaped
as they realised what had happened.
"We've been tricked!" the tall one
groaned, his head in his hands.

"Sorry," Kirsty said cheerfully, as she
helped up the goblin who'd fallen over.

"But you shouldn't take things that don't belong to you – and you definitely shouldn't try to cheat by using magic!"

As the goblins launched into furious bickering about whose fault it was that they no longer had the clef, Kirsty skipped off to find Vanessa and Rachel, with a big smile on her face. They'd found the clef, and now everyone's dance steps would fall into place!

Later that evening, Kirsty and Rachel filed onto the stage with the other children from the dance class. When they'd met for the rehearsal at six o'clock, Vanessa had used her dance magic to ensure that *everyone* danced brilliantly to Sasha's routine, including Sasha herself. They were all so good that it had been impossible for Sasha and Tamara to choose just a few children to dance on stage. In the end, they had all been chosen, and the stage was very full.

"It's a shame those boys didn't come back," Kirsty heard Sasha saying to Tamara. "They were fabulous."

Kirsty grinned at Rachel. They could guess why the 'boys' hadn't come back – they must be in big trouble with Jack Frost for losing the magic dance clef!

The lights dimmed on stage, and everyone stood in their starting positions. Then, as the opening notes of *Let's Dance* played, a roar of applause went up from the audience, giving Rachel goosebumps. She couldn't believe she was here on stage at the Rainspell Music Festival, about to dance with Kirsty in front of thousands of people!

"I'd be nervous if it wasn't for you, Vanessa," Kirsty whispered. "I'm glad you're here with us!"

Vanessa, who was tucked inside Kirsty's pocket, grinned. "I wouldn't miss it for anything," she said.

"And now that I have my clef back, my dance steps magic will make sure everyone dances like a dream!"

As Sasha launched into the first verse, the girls stopped talking and danced along with everyone else. Rachel caught a glimpse of her parents in the audience, clapping and waving, and felt as if she might burst with happiness and pride.

"This has been the best day EVER," Kirsty sighed when the song finally came to an end, and the audience cheered.

"I know," Rachel agreed, grinning breathlessly. "Three fairy adventures in a single day – that's a new record, Kirsty. And with four clefs left to find, who knows what will happen tomorrow?"

Kirsty smiled. "I can't wait to find out," she said happily.

Now Kirsty and Rachel
must help...

Miley the Stylist Fairy

Read on for a sneak peek...

"What's that noise?" Rachel murmured sleepily. She could hear a steady *pitter-patter* sound on the roof of the tent above her. Yawning, Rachel sat up in her sleeping bag. At the same moment, her best friend Kirsty stirred and opened her eyes.

"Oh, it's *raining!*" Rachel exclaimed, suddenly realising what the noise was.

Kirsty sat up, too. "Is that thunder?" she asked a little nervously as a loud rumbling echoed through the tent.

Rachel laughed. "No, that's my dad

snoring in the other bedroom!" she explained. Scrambling out of her sleeping bag, she went over to the tent's main entrance. Kirsty followed, and together the two girls peered out.

The site of the Rainspell Island Music Festival was awash with heavy rain. The sky was dark and threatening, and the grassy fields where the tents, stages and pop stars' trailers had been set up were already turning to mud.

"What a shame!" Kirsty remarked, "Especially when we had such brilliant weather yesterday."

"It doesn't matter whether it's sunny or rainy, though, does it?" Rachel reminded her. "We've still *got* to keep looking for the Pop Star Fairies' magical clefs!"

Kirsty nodded. "I wonder which

fairy we'll be helping today?" she said.

When the girls had arrived on Rainspell the day before, they'd discovered that Jack Frost and his goblins had been up to their tricks again. This time they'd stolen the Pop Star Fairies' magical musical clefs...

Read Miley the Stylist Fairy to find out what adventures are in store for Kirsty and Rachel!

Meet the
Pop Star Fairies

Kirsty and Rachel have to save Rainspell Island Music Festival after Jack Frost steals the Pop Star Fairies' musical clef necklaces!

www.rainbowmagicbooks.co.uk

RAINBOW magic

Meet the fairies, play games
and get sneak peeks at
the latest books!

www.rainbowmagicbooks.co.uk

There's fairy fun for everyone on
our wonderful website.
You'll find great activities, competitions, stories and
fairy profiles, and also a special newsletter.

Get 30% off all Rainbow Magic books at
www.rainbowmagicbooks.co.uk

Enter the code RAINBOW at the checkout.
Offer ends 31 December 2012.

Offer valid in United Kingdom and Republic of Ireland only.

Competition!

Here's a friend who Kirsty and Rachel met in an earlier story. Use the clues below to help you guess her name. When you have enjoyed all seven of the Pop Star Fairies books, arrange the first letters of each mystery fairy's name to make a special word, then send us the answer!

CLUES

1. I'm one of the Magical Animal fairies.

2. My special friend breathes fire.

3. I have a funky afro hairstyle.

The fairy's name is _ _ _ _ _ _ the _ _ _ _ _ _ Fairy

We will put all of the correct entries into a draw and select one winner to receive a special Pop Star Fairies goody bag. Your name will also be featured in a forthcoming Rainbow Magic story!

Enter online now at www.rainbowmagicbooks.co.uk

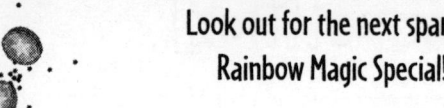